Mar/94

The Artist
By John Bianchi

Bungalo Books

Written by John Bianchi
Illustrated by John Bianchi
Copyright 1993 by Bungalo Books

Canadian Cataloguing in Publication Data

Bianchi, John
   The Artist

ISBN 0-921285-29-9 (bound)   ISBN 0-921285-28-0 (pbk.)

1. Title.

PS8553.I26A78 1993   jC813'.54   C93-090379-X
PZ7.B43Ar 1993

Published in Canada by: Trade Distribution:
Bungalo Books   Firefly Books Ltd.
Box 129   250 Sparks Avenue
Newburgh, Ontario   Willowdale, Ontario
KOK 2S0   M2H 2S4

Co-published in U.S.A. by: Printed in Canada by:
Firefly Books (U.S.) Inc.   Friesen Printers
Ellicott Station   Altona, Manitoba
P.O. Box 1338
Buffalo, New York 14205

In memory of Jean Richard
1939 - 1991

and to Lupcia and Ian,
who provided the inspiration

Even when he was very young, Amelio loved to paint. Though his paintbox was small, his imagination was immense, and he would often work for hours painting remarkable pictures while dreaming of a life as a great artist.

When he grew older, Amelio loved to go to the park to study the famous artists of the day. He would often make notes and drawings in a small sketchbook that was with him wherever he went.

Sometimes, he would visit Henri Maltese, known for his legendary experiments with colour.

Other times, he would stop for a chat with Dame Emily van Borzoi, whose powerful landscapes were filled with magnificent light. And he would never miss a chance to watch Camille Briard, whose use of radical composition had turned the art world upside down.

Amelio could not wait to grow up and follow in the footsteps of his heroes. Someday, he, too, would be a painter of great landscapes.

But luck was not with Amelio. Times turned tough, and each member of the family had to help out.

"And what will you do?" asked Amelio's mother.

"I will paint faces in the little park by the Gorgonzola Bridge," said Amelio.

And that is exactly what he did. In fact, he became well known for the glorious rainbows he would paint on the cheeks of his young customers.

But this left no time for painting great landscapes.

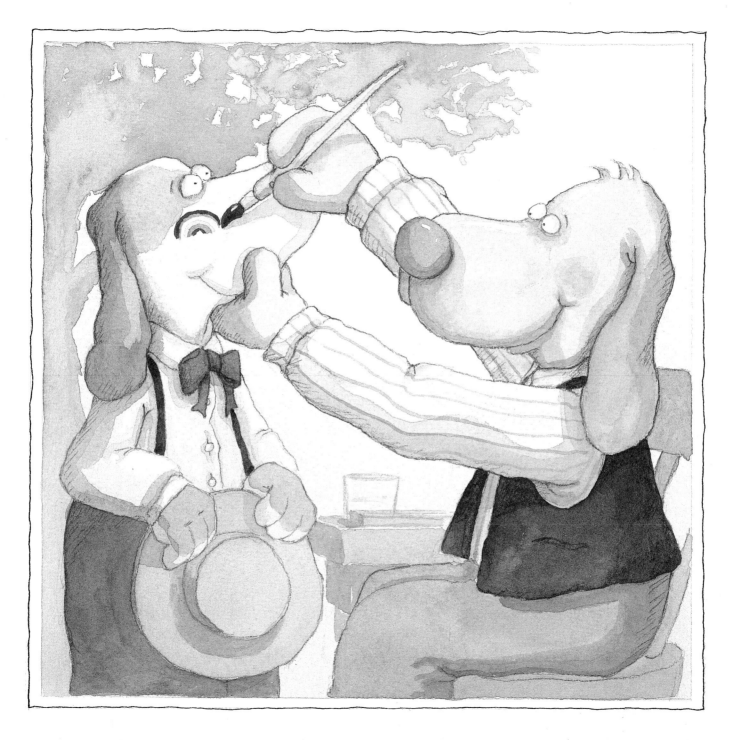

When he was older, Amelio decided to attend art school.

"And how will you pay for your education?" asked Amelio's father.

"I will sketch portraits of the ladies and gentlemen in the town square," replied Amelio.

And that is exactly what he did.

While he was at art school, Amelio fell in love with the beautiful Lemonjello.

"Will you marry me?" asked Amelio one day while they were dancing at the café.

"Of course!" replied Lemonjello.

"And how will you two support yourselves?" asked their parents when they had been told the news.

"I will create fashion designs for all the famous dress salons," said Lemonjello.

"And I will make posters for the town's opera house," replied Amelio.

Amelio and Lemonjello hoped to have a large family, and when the little ones arrived, Amelio took an extra job working nights at the Provolone Sign Company.

Now, the painting of great landscapes was nothing more than a distant memory that would sometimes visit Amelio while he was inscribing an especially ornate letter on one of his signs . . .

. . . or changing a diaper on one of his puppies.

Whenever the town needed an artist, Amelio was always there.

He designed packages for the Presto Pasta Company, fashioned greeting cards for the Mama Mia Stationery Store and sketched courtroom scenes for the town newspaper. He even helped a local architect design affordable houses.

And so went the artist's life. Happily distracted by the joys of his family and his work, Amelio had no chance to create great landscapes.

Only in his later years did Amelio finally find time to paint. On sunny days, he would visit the park to work on his landscapes . . . but would usually end up entertaining his many grandpups.

One day, when he was was quite old, Amelio fell gravely ill. A doctor was summoned, and his family gathered around him. All knew that Amelio was not long for this world. Some started to cry.

"Please," said Amelio, "do not cry for me. I have had a good, long life and have been able to watch you all grow up. I only wish I had had more time to spend with the beautiful Lemonjello and maybe a few more moments to paint pictures of this wonderful land."

The old artist died that night and was immediately escorted to heaven by an angel. After a hot bath and a chocolate cappuccino, Amelio was given a new robe, a fresh set of wings and a halo. Then he was brought before God.

"My staff and I have watched your life with much interest," said God. "And since you have led an honest and kindly life and have always cared for your family, we have decided to grant you a permanent place in heaven.

"Now, the first thing you'll need is a job – we like to keep our new angels as busy as possible. Let's see . . ."

God started reading through his job file.

"We have openings for a face painter: 'must have previous experience.' A portrait artist: 'please show samples of recent work.' And a sign painter: 'must be able to spell big words.'

"You may have your choice of any of these fine heavenly occupations."

"Thank you, God," said Amelio. "I am most honoured. But would you have an opening for a landscape artist?"

"Let me look again," said God. "Well, there is nothing like that available at this time. But why don't I create a job for you in the Glorious Sunrise Department? Would you like that?"

"I would love it," said Amelio.

"Then you shall have it!" said God. "But before you start, would you paint one of your famous rainbows on my face?"

"Of course!" replied Amelio.

And so, after a lifetime of hard work, Amelio was at last able to create great landscapes. And one morning, if you are up early enough . . .

. . . you may have the good fortune to see some of his fine work.

THE AUTHOR

John Bianchi is an author/illustrator with almost 20 children's books to his credit. His best known works include *Princess Frownsalot, The Swine Snafu, Penelope Penguin: The Incredibly Good Baby* and *Snowed In At Pokeweed Public School.*

His books with creative partner Frank B. Edwards include *Mortimer Mooner Stopped Taking a Bath* and *Snow: Learning For The Fun Of It.*

The pair formed Bungalo Books in 1986 and gave up serious employment shortly after so that they could pursue their love of children's books on a full-time basis.